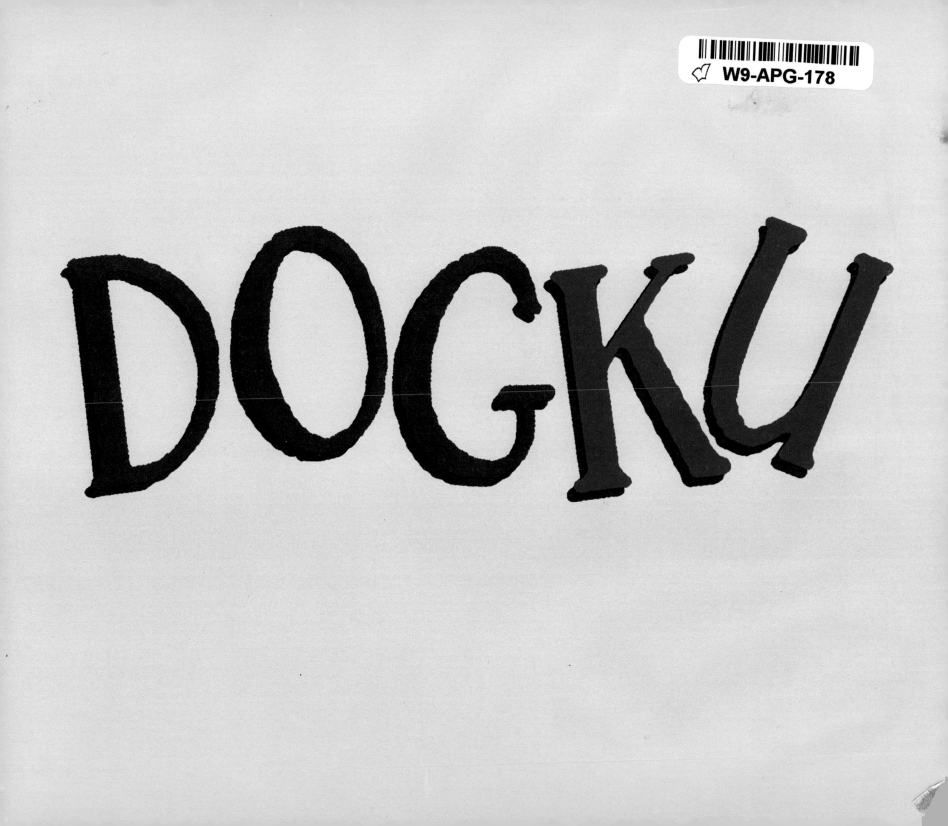

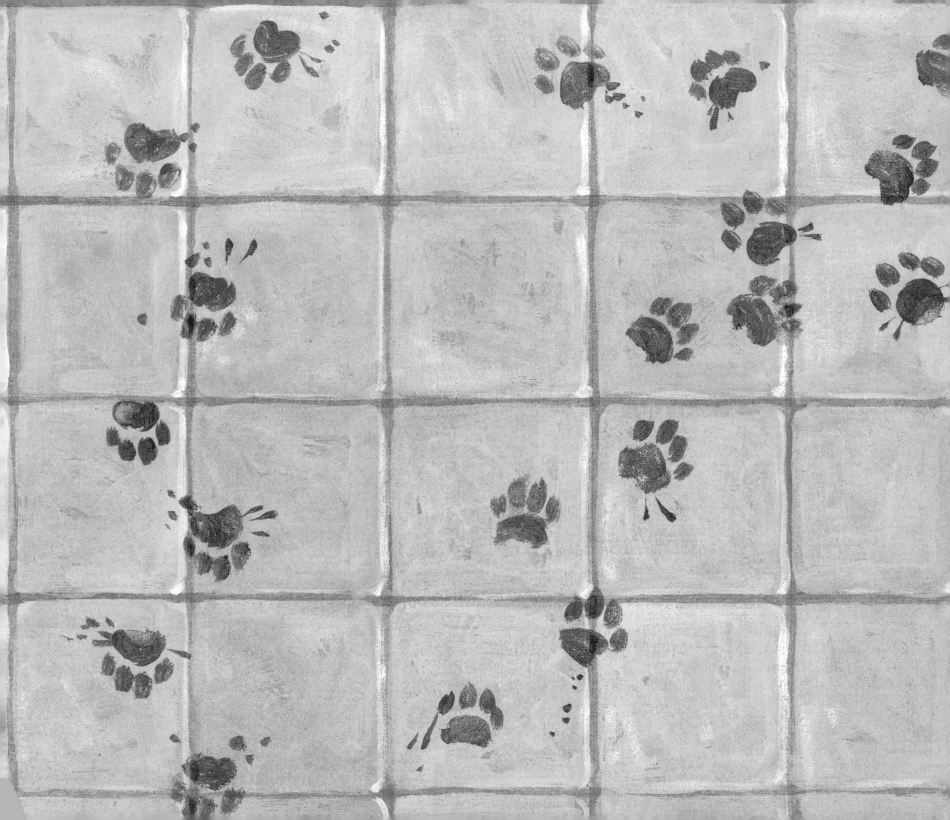

Andrew Clements
DOGKU

ILLUSTRATED BY TIM BOWERS

SCHOLASTIC INC.
New York Toronto London Auckland Sydney
Mexico City New Delhi Hong Kong Buenos Aires

There on the back steps,
the eyes of a hungry dog.
Will she shut the door?

First food, then a bath.
The food was a lot more fun.
Still, it all feels good.

Morning brings children.
Hugs, licks, barking, and laughing.
Warmer than sunshine.

A dog needs a name.
Rags? Mutt? Pooch? No, not Rover.
Mooch. Yes, Mooch! Perfect.

Loud, fast, and crazy.
Food, coats, then the front door slams.
Mooch hates the school bus.

First, "Arf, arf!" Then, "Woof!"
Soon, "Arf, arf!" Then, "Woof! Woof, woof!"
Mooch has nice neighbors.

Nose out the window,
ears flapping, hair pushed straight back.
Adventures in smell.

The house is quiet.
No kids, no mom, and no food.
What's a dog to do?

Chew on dirty socks.
Roll around in week-old trash.
Ahhh . . . that's much better.

Squirrel sits in tree.
Mooch sits below, looking up.
Who has more patience?

Sun all morning long.
A deep, cool drink of water.
Shade all afternoon.

Scratch, sniff, eat, yawn, nap.
Dreams of rabbits and running.
Could life be sweeter?

The sound of children—
that's what was missing all day.
Mooch loves the school bus.

Family meeting.

There are words and words and words.

Did someone say "pound"?

Dad puts on his coat.
And then the sound of a car.
It doesn't look good.

It's the car again.
And then footsteps at the door.
Will this be good-bye?

A new doggy bed!
Food, a bowl, a squeaky toy!
Mooch has found his home.